Dear Parents and Educators,

Welcome to Penguin Young Readers! As parents and educators, you know that each child develops at his or her own pace—in terms of speech, critical thinking, and, of course, reading. Penguin Young Readers recognizes this fact. As a result, each Penguin Young Readers book is assigned a traditional easy-to-read level (1–4) as well as a Guided Reading Level (A–P). Both of these systems will help you choose the right book for your child. Please refer to the back of each book for specific leveling information. Penguin Young Readers features esteemed authors and illustrators, stories about favorite characters, fascinating nonfiction, and more!

Max & Ruby: Max's Lunch

LEVEL **2**

GUIDED
READING
LEVEL **F**

This book is perfect for a **Progressing Reader** who:
- can figure out unknown words by using picture and context clues;
- can recognize beginning, middle, and ending sounds;
- can make and confirm predictions about what will happen in the text; and
- can distinguish between fiction and nonfiction.

Here are some **activities** you can do during and after reading this book:
- Picture Clues: Use the pictures to tell the story. Have the child go through the book, retelling the story just by looking at the pictures.
- Rhyming Words: On a separate piece of paper, make a list of all the rhyming words in this story. For example, *bunch* rhymes with *crunch*, so write those two words next to each other.

Remember, sharing the love of reading with a child is the best gift you can give!

—Sarah Fabiny, Editorial Director
Penguin Young Readers program

*Penguin Young Readers are leveled by independent reviewers applying the standards developed by Irene Fountas and Gay Su Pinnell in *Matching Books to Readers: Using Leveled Books in Guided Reading*, Heinemann, 1999.

For my son, Taylor—AG

PENGUIN YOUNG READERS
An Imprint of Penguin Random House LLC

Penguin supports copyright. Copyright fuels creativity, encourages diverse voices,
promotes free speech, and creates a vibrant culture. Thank you for buying an authorized edition
of this book and for complying with copyright laws by not reproducing, scanning, or distributing any
part of it in any form without permission. You are supporting writers and allowing Penguin to
continue to publish books for every reader.

Cover art by Rosemary Wells

Library of Congress Cataloging-in-Publication Data is available.

ISBN 9780515157376 (pbk)   10 9 8 7 6 5 4 3 2 1
ISBN 9780515157383 (hc)   10 9 8 7 6 5 4 3 2 1

PENGUIN YOUNG READERS

LEVEL 2

PROGRESSING READER

Max & Ruby!

Max's Lunch

by Rosemary Wells
illustrated by Andrew Grey

Penguin Young Readers
An Imprint of Penguin Random House

In Max's lunch is a great big bunch of yogurt, carrots, and apples—

crunch!

Max just can't wait to eat it all.

The lunch boxes go in the hall.

Max washes up.

His hands are grubby.

But Max's lunch is not

in his cubby.

"Where's my lunch?

It's gone away!

8

Now I have nothing to eat

today!"

Max looks under the table
and chairs.

He looks in the closet

under the stairs.

There's no lunch

in the turtle terrarium.

There's no lunch

in the fish aquarium.

There's no lunch

on the closet floor.

There's nothing at all

in the teacher's drawer.

"I'm so thirsty, and hungry, too!"

Says Max, "What is a bunny to do?"

Ruby says, "Don't make a fuss!

Do you think you left it on the bus?"

19

Lily says, "I will share my lunch with you.

I have lots of grapes

and blueberries, too."

Max and Lily start to share

her lunch.

"Wait!" says Ruby.

"I have a hunch!"

The school bus is parked

under the trees.

Ruby asks the driver,

"Help us, please?"

"There may be a lunch box
on seat number three.
Do you think you could take
a look and see?"

The bus driver finds Max's lunch
on the seat.

Carrots and apples, what a treat!

"See, Max," says Ruby.

"You were being silly!

Now go and share your lunch

with Lily."

Max and Lily eat everything up.

Carrots, apples, and a yogurt cup.

"We'll eat up my grapes
and blueberries, and then,"
says Lily, "we'll never be
hungry again!"